Karma

The Price of Actions and the Fire of Hell

ZAKIR JAWED BHATTI

Copyright © 2025 by Zakir Jawed Bhatti

All rights reserved. No part of this publication may be reproduced, stored or transmitted in any form or by any means, photocopying, scanning, electronic, mechanical, recording, or otherwise without written permission from the publisher.

ISBN: 978-1-0691981-5-0

To my Mentor,

With deepest gratitude for your unwavering belief in my writing. Your guidance, encouragement, and inspiration have been my guiding light.

Table of Contents

Chapter 1: Shadows of Al Jazab 5

Chapter 2: The Scent of Dread.. 12

Chapter 3: Whispers from the Depths............................ 19

Chapter 4: Bound by the Past 25

Chapter 5: The Father in the Shadows........................... 35

Chapter 6: When the Sky weeps 42

Chapter 7: Hell is Coming 47

Chapter 8: Descent into Hell 55

Chapter 9: A Hell of a Misunderstanding...................... 65

Chapter 10: Vengeance from Hell 80

Chapter 11: Hellbound... 86

Chapter 1

Shadows of Al Jazab

Haider sat at the edge of the bed, his eyes fixed on Heidi as she packed her suitcase with a careful yet determined precision.

The soft rustle of clothes being folded and stuffed into the red bag was the only sound in the room, save for the occasional breath Haider took as he watched her.

She was beautiful—there was no denying that. But today, the beauty of her face, the steady grace with which she moved, felt distant to him.

It was as if the woman he loved had been replaced by someone he no longer recognized.

"Please, Heidi," Haider's voice cracked, his usually calm demeanor showing signs of strain. "You can't go there."

Heidi didn't look at him, her focus entirely on her task. Her hands moved quickly but precisely, as though each item was a life raft, packing away pieces of her that she couldn't leave behind.

"I have to go, Haider. People are dying—men, women, children—because of this disease, and no one is helping them."

Haider's voice grew more urgent as the words tumbling out in a desperate plea. "Heidi, I know you're a doctor, but this... this is different. It's not just the disease. There's no infrastructure, no sanitation. It's chaos. It's dangerous, and you're walking right into it. You could die there."

Heidi paused for a moment, looking at him over her shoulder, her expression a mix of frustration and pity. "And you think I don't know that? I'm not blind to the risks, Haider. But if I don't go, who will? Who else will help those people? The doctors from nearby cities are too scared. There's no one left who will step up."

Haider's chest tightened; his heart thundering in his ears. He stood up and walked toward her, his steps heavy with the weight of his emotions. "Why should it be you? Why not someone else?"

Heidi's hands stopped moving as she turned to face him, her face soft but unwavering. "Because they're too afraid to take the risk. They see the danger and they back away. But I'm not like that, Haider. I can't just stand by when people are suffering."

Haider's face grew pale. His eyes darted from the suitcase to her face. "But I love you, Heidi. I can't lose you. Please."

Heidi reached for her bag and zipped it closed with a decisive motion. "And if you love me, Haider, you'll understand why I have to do this." She stepped closer, her fingers gently brushing his. "This is my duty."

He reached out, his hands trembling slightly as he took her hands in his. "Please, Heidi. You're all I have. Don't leave me.

"She gazed at him with a mixture of sadness and resolve. "If you love me, you won't try to stop me. You'll support me. Let me do this."

A long silence stretched between them, a chasm neither could bridge. Haider could feel his heart breaking, each moment dragging him further into the abyss of fear and helplessness. Finally, he whispered, barely audible, "I can't do this. I can't let you go."

Heidi's eyes softened, but there was no trace of hesitation. She squeezed his hands one last time and released them. "I'm going, Haider. I have to."

As the days passed, Haider's mind remained fixed on Heidi's departure, the weight of her absence pressing on him like a suffocating force.

The worst part was not just the fear for her safety—it was the knowledge that there was nothing he could do to change her mind.

Haider entered the bathroom after another long day in the field and stood under the shower, letting the hot water cascade over him.

His muscles, taut from days of tension and lack of sleep, slowly began to relax under the pressure of the stream. But his mind raced.

Every thought led back to Heidi, and every scenario he imagined only made the situation more unbearable.

The shower did little to quiet his racing heart. He finally turned off the water, stepped out, and entered the prayer room, hoping the quiet ritual would bring him peace.

Kneeling on the prayer mat, Haider lowered his forehead to the cool fabric, his palms pressed firmly into the ground. Silence enveloped him—comforting and suffocating.

His breath came in soft, measured bursts, but his mind was far from calm. It was filled with images of Heidi—her smile, her laughter, her determination.

His prayer was soft, almost a whisper. "Allah, please protect her. Please keep her safe. Please bring her back to me."

He prostrated again, and then sat back on his heels. He rose and looked at the picture of them both on the wall—a photo from a happier time, before the reality of their lives had torn them apart. He closed his eyes and reached out to touch the frame. A single tear escaped down his cheek.

The next morning, Haider woke up in a cold sweat. The dream had been vivid—too vivid. His pulse raced as he sat up in bed, the remnants of the nightmare clinging to him like a thick fog.

He had seen the aftermath of an attack in Al Jazab: a man and woman, burnt beyond recognition, their charred bodies lying on the ground beside the sign for the town. Flames had consumed everything, and the stench of burning flesh had filled the air, choking him with its heaviness.

Haider gasped for breath, clutching his chest as he tried to steady himself.

His body refused to move at first, as if the weight of the dream had locked him in place. He fought to breathe, to scream, but it was as if the air itself had been stolen from him.

KARMA

Finally, after what seemed like an eternity, Haider managed to move. He stumbled to the kitchen, his legs shaky as he grabbed a glass of water. The cold liquid burned as it went down his throat, but it did little to extinguish the fire of fear that blazed in his chest. Later that morning, Haider sat at the dining table, mechanically eating his breakfast, but his mind was elsewhere. The news report on the television was a distant, disjointed sound.

"…The fifth deadly blaze in Al Jazab," the reporter said, her voice grim. Haider's heart skipped a beat as the images of destruction flashed on the screen.

Fire fighters fought to control the flames, but the damage had already been done. The reporter continued. "The cause of the fire is under investigation. We've recovered ten bodies so far."

Haider felt the world tilt beneath him. He had heard the rumours of violence and unrest in Al Jazab, but this… this was something else. It was more than just a dangerous place. It was a place of death, a place where hope went to die. His gaze fell to the burning building on the screen, the chaos that unfolded there. "I told her not to go…" Haider muttered under his breath. "But she never listens."

***

As Haider drove through the streets of Al Jazab later that day, the town's haunting emptiness seemed to swallow him whole. The once-vibrant community had become a wasteland of destruction and despair.

As he passed a burnt-out police station, a surge of nausea hit him. His stomach twisted as memories of his nightmare resurfaced. The images of the burned bodies—the horror—had become all too real.

Then, out of nowhere, a young girl about six years old, darted in front of his car. He slammed on the brakes, the tires screeching in protest, his heart pounding as the car came to a halt just inches from her frail form.

He stepped out of the car, his legs unsteady as he approached her. The girl was sickly thin, her skin a pale yellow.

Haider's stomach dropped as he saw the horrifyingly gaunt face that looked back at him. There was something unnatural about her—something wrong.

"What are you doing here?" he asked, his voice barely above a whisper.

A girl's face was grotesque, almost inhuman, the skin stretched tight across her bones. Haider's breath caught in his throat as he instinctively closed his eyes, the terror overwhelming him.

When he opened them again, girl had disappeared, leaving him alone in the empty street.

As he arrived at the hospital later that day, Haider's heart felt heavy with the weight of his thoughts.

The town of Al Jazab had become a nightmare—a place where humanity was swallowed whole, a place where even hope seemed to die.

He leaned against the car, staring at the hospital in the distance, the sense of foreboding growing stronger by the second.

In his voiceover, Haider's words echoed, heavy with realization: "When I worked as a journalist, I thought the outside world was the worst. But now, standing here, I understand. This town... this place... it's the true hell."

And Heidi, the woman he loved, had chosen to come here.

Chapter 2

The Scent of Dread

The hospital loomed in the distance, its bleak exterior an unwelcome reminder of the past. As Haider stepped inside, the heavy door closed behind him with a quiet but firm thud, sealing him off from the world outside. The air was thick with the sterile scent of antiseptic and something older, almost musty.

The dim lights overhead flickered intermittently, casting long shadows on the cracked tiles that lined the walls. The hallway stretched endlessly before him, its oppressive silence only broken by the echo of his footsteps.

Behind him, the young girl whom he had seen earlier on the road walked quietly, her footsteps barely audible. Haider glanced over his shoulder, but the moment he did, the door slammed shut with a jarring sound that sent a shiver down his spine. He turned forward again, but the emptiness of the corridor made his heart race faster than it should have. There was something unsettling about this place, a presence that seemed to seep from the walls.

Before he could even begin to process the unease crawling up his spine, something else caught his attention— a noise, soft but distinct. A thud. He stopped, looking down at his luggage where something had fallen to the floor.

He bent to retrieve it, but as his hand touched the ground, he realized it wasn't the sound of something falling from his bag—it had come from somewhere else. The noise was far too sharp, purposeful to be anything ordinary.

He glanced down the hallway, expecting to see a shadow or figure lurking in the distance. But there was nothing. Not a single soul in sight.

Young girl was gone. She had vanished. Haider's breath hitched in his chest, and before he could call out to her, a dark shape appeared from the shadows, moving too quickly for him to comprehend. It was almost as if the darkness itself had taken shape. A figure—tall, indistinct—lunged from behind him, dragging her into the dark recesses of the hallway.

Haider froze, his mind racing. What had just happened? His body tensed, a sickening chill running through him as he instinctively spun around, searching the hallway for any trace of her, but it was as though she had never been there at all. The hallway was empty once again.

A low, metallic creak echoed from above, and his eyes darted upward. Nothing. No sound except for the distant hum of fluorescent lights. He stood there, breathless, unable to process what he had just witnessed. Had he imagined it? No. He knew what he had seen.

He pushed forward, forcing his legs to move despite the weight of his growing unease. The longer he stayed in this hospital, the stranger it seemed. The walls were stained with years of neglect—cracked tiles, peeling paint, and an oppressive sense of abandonment clung to the very air.

As he wandered deeper, the light seemed to fade, leaving him in a shadowy, disorienting maze.

He passed the waiting room, and for a moment, he stopped, staring through the grimy glass at the nurse's station. The counter was a mess of clutter, papers scattered and abandoned, a small stack of old magazines curling at the edges.

Behind it stood a woman, smiling too brightly for someone in such a decrepit place. She was cheerful, but her eyes... her eyes seemed distant, unfocused.

"Welcome!" she chirped, though her voice didn't quite match the rest of her demeanor. "How can I help you?"

Haider hesitated. "I need to see Dr. Heidi," he said, his voice edged with impatience.

The woman's smile didn't falter. "Please wait a moment. She'll be right with you."

Haider sat down on one of the uncomfortable chairs, running his hands over the worn fabric, the tension in his body building with each passing second. The silence around him was unnerving. A few patients sat quietly in the corner, their eyes wide, never meeting his gaze. A few nurses drifted by, but they moved like automatons—eyes glazed over, their steps quick, avoiding any contact.

He barely noticed the time pass before he spotted Dr. Heidi moving through the hallway.

She was walking briskly, talking to a group of nurses, and it looked like they were carrying something in a gurney—someone, though Haider couldn't tell who.

As he made his way toward her, a soft murmur broke through the silence. Nurses rushed by him, a patient in tow. Haider froze.

Haider watched them disappear into the ICU. He followed, drawn to the doors that loomed ahead. They opened as Haider stood on the threshold. Inside, the harsh beeping of monitors and the muted shuffle of medical staff filled the air. Dr. Heidi and a team of nurses were busy around a bed, turning a patient onto her stomach to relieve the pressure on her lungs. The woman on the bed was pale, her face twisted in discomfort, tubes trailing from her back, keeping her alive in a way that seemed almost unnatural.

Haider felt his stomach churn as he watched them work. His gaze shifted, and he noticed an older nurse standing behind him, watching him with a cold expression.

"What are you doing here?" the nurse, Jazmin, asked in a clipped tone. "No one is allowed in here—only medical staff. Please, go sit down."

Haider took a step back, his throat tight. He nodded and retreated from the door, but his mind was already whirling. Why was this place so wrong?

The patients were so still, their faces too blank, their eyes too vacant. He couldn't shake the feeling that something wasn't just off—it was wrong in a way he couldn't explain.

Minutes later, he found himself back in the waiting room, slumping into a chair. His eyelids grew heavy, the exhaustion from his journey creeping up on him like a weight he couldn't fight. He leaned back, his body still tense, but the relentless pull of sleep overtook him.

When he woke, it was with a start. He blinked, disoriented, but the room was empty. It felt like no time had passed at all, but somehow everything had changed. His heartbeat quickened as he looked around. The quiet had deepened, now more unnerving than peaceful.

Haider pushed himself out of the chair and stood, looking down the hallway. He moved toward the ICU again, his curiosity getting the better of him. This time, there was no one in the room. No nurses. No patients. The machines hummed quietly, but there was an emptiness that swallowed the space. He knocked on the glass, his voice rising in frustration. "Heidi!?"

There was no response. His pulse quickened, and the hairs on the back of his neck stood up. The silence was suffocating. Turning, he stumbled into the next room. Blood. Drops of it were scattered on the floor, leading him to the next room, where the walls were streaked with crimson. His breath caught in his throat, and he reached for his phone, but the signal was gone. Panic surged through him as he moved through the rooms, each one more disturbing than the last.

"HEIDI!" he screamed, but the words seemed to vanish into the cold, sterile air. He ran into the hallway, gasping for breath. When he turned, he saw a nurse at the far end, walking briskly.

Haider didn't hesitate—he followed her, desperate for answers. But when he reached her, Jazmin stopped him before he could enter the nurse's station.

"This is the nurse station," she said, coldly. "Families of patients aren't allowed in here."

Before Haider could protest, Jazmin gave him a firm shove, pushing him back into the hallway. And then, as if on cue, he saw her. Heidi was standing just behind him, her eyes filled with a strange calm. A chill ran down his spine. "Heidi, there's something wrong here. I saw—".

But before he could finish, Heidi's hand gently touched his shoulder. "What happened?" she asked, her voice soft but edged with concern.

"There's this little girl," Haider stammered, his mind struggling to find the words. "She's been—she's here somewhere. In the hospital."

Heidi's expression remained unchanged. "There is no one here, Haider. I think you're just tired from the journey. You need to rest."

His mind raced. "Where were you? What happened in the ICU? There was blood everywhere."

Heidi sighed, a slight frown tugging at her lips. "I don't know what you're talking about." She paused for a moment, her eyes soft but distant. "I think you just need to rest. Let's go to your room. You can tell me everything later."

Heidi's calmness felt like a weight pressing down on him. She smiled at him, but there was something off about her eyes—a glimmer of something unreadable, as if she was a stranger in her own skin.

Haider's heart hammered in his chest as he followed her down the hallway. The strange sensation of being trapped in a nightmare lingered in his mind.

Something was wrong. Something he couldn't explain. But as he followed Heidi, the oppressive silence of the hospital seemed to close in on him.

Chapter 3

Whispers from the Depths

Haider stepped out of the hospital, his breath a cloud in the cold night air. He pulled a cigarette from his pocket, fingers trembling slightly as he lit it.

The flame flickered, briefly casting his tired face in orange light before it was swallowed by the shadows. Behind him, the hospital loomed, its towering walls barely visible in the darkness. It felt like something more than just a building—a monolith, a thing of dread that had outlasted times itself.

He leaned against a crumbling stone wall, feeling the bite of the cold seep through his coat. But it wasn't the temperature that made him shiver—it was the presence of the hospital. Something was wrong here. It wasn't just the creaking floors or the flickering lights; it was as though the building itself was waiting for something. Watching him. The hospital wasn't just a place—it was alive.

He drew another drag from the cigarette, the smoke swirling in the thick night air, but it did little to calm the storm brewing in his chest. His thoughts kept returning to the same question: Why did this place still haunt him after all these years?

He pulled out his phone, dialing Azan's number with quick, practiced motions. It rang twice before his friend answered.

"Hey, man. How's everything?" Azan's voice was casual, but Haider could hear the underlying concern.

"It's... fine, I guess," Haider replied, his voice flat. "You wouldn't believe this place. It hasn't changed at all—still feels like something out of a nightmare."

He glanced back at the hospital, its dim lights flickering ominously in the dark. "I'll talk to Heidi and head back soon. Just need to clear my head for a bit."

Azan paused. "Did you see your father yet?"

The question hit Haider like a punch to the gut. He stiffened, a cold wave of irritation rushing through him. His father.

The man who had left him years ago, the one whose absence still hung like a heavy cloud over everything he did.

"No," Haider replied quickly, his voice colder than he intended. "I heard he left town a while ago. And I'm not interested in seeing him. Not now."

Azan didn't push the issue, but Haider could hear the hesitation in his voice. "Alright. Just take care, okay? Let me know when you're coming back."

"I will," Haider muttered, ending the call with a sharp swipe. The emptiness of the night pressed in on him. He shoved the phone into his pocket and took another drag, trying to steady his racing thoughts. The chill in the air was nothing compared to the knot in his stomach.

His feet scraped against the gravel as he walked back toward the hospital; something was off. He had always felt uneasy here, but tonight, the tension was palpable. The building seemed to breathe with a life of its own.

Inside, Heidi's room was dim. The only light came from the flickering fluorescent bulb overhead. Haider had been waiting for what felt like hours. His thoughts were scattered, his mind reeling with fragmented memories. The place was starting to get to him.

The unsettling noises, the strange feeling of being watched—it was as though the hospital itself was trying to push him to the edge of his sanity.

Then, Heidi stepped into the room.

She was pale, her hair tangled, her eyes unfocused, as if she were still half-dreaming. Haider froze. A wave of unease washed over him, cold and sudden. Something was wrong—something deep and primal. He couldn't quite put his finger on it, but his instincts screamed that she was no longer the person he had known.

Heidi moved closer, her hand raised high, the scalpel gripped tightly in her fingers, its blade glistening with blood. She held it steady, the sharp edge reflecting the dim light, a clear threat.

"Please, Heidi... put down the scalpel," Haider's voice trembled, a mixture of fear and desperation in his words. His eyes were fixed on the blade, every nerve in his body screaming for him to escape, but he couldn't move. He swallowed hard, trying to steady his breath. "Put it down."

Heidi didn't respond. Her fingers tightened around the handle, her expression dark and unwavering. She stepped forward, slowly, deliberately, her eyes locked on him with a cold, unnatural intensity.

Haider's heart pounded in his chest as he took a step back. His voice cracked as he pleaded again, "Heidi, please... stop. Don't do this."

"I will kill everyone," she hissed, her voice guttural and alien, like something not human. The words vibrated with malice, echoing in the hollow silence of the room.

Haider's blood turned to ice. He couldn't move. His body refused to listen to his mind, and the room seemed to close in around him, suffocating him. And then, without thinking, he bolted. His legs moved before his brain could catch up, his feet pounding against the cold, sterile tiles as he sprinted down the hallway.

He didn't know how far he ran—just that he couldn't stop. The silence that followed him made his skin crawl, each step louder than the last, echoing through the empty corridors. But no matter how far he went, it felt like the hospital was stretching endlessly, swallowing him whole.

Finally, he burst through the doors and into the night. The world outside was eerily silent, and the road stretched ahead of him, desolate and empty.

There was no one. No cars. No sounds. Just the cold and the emptiness pressing in.

"Help! Somebody, help me!" Haider screamed, his voice raw and desperate, but it was swallowed by the stillness.

KARMA

His heart hammered in his chest, his breath coming in ragged gasps. He turned and ran, feet hitting the gravel, but the road seemed endless. No matter how fast he ran, he didn't get any closer to anything.

Then he saw them. A group of people stood at the side of the road, staring down at their phones. At first, Haider thought they might help, but as he got closer, he noticed their faces—blank.

Vacant. Unmoving. They didn't acknowledge him. They didn't even blink. Their eyes were wide, glassy.

A chill ran through him. Something wasn't right.

And then, through the fog, they appeared.

Two figures, walking toward him, slow and deliberate. Their bodies were burned beyond recognition—charred, blackened, the skin sloughing off like melted wax. Their faces were a grotesque mess of melted flesh, eyes hollow and unseeing.

They didn't speak. Didn't need to. Their silence spoke louder than any words could.

Haider's heart skipped a beat. The world around him blurred. Panic surged. His breath came in shallow gasps. He needed to run. But his legs were heavy, like they were made of stone.

And then familiar young girl appeared.

Her small hand gripped his arm, icy cold, sending a shock through his body.

"You again" Haider whispered, his voice trembling with fear. "Where did you come from? Why... why do you keep appearing? What do you want?"

She didn't answer. She couldn't. Blood began to pour from her mouth, thick and dark, dripping down her chin in an endless stream. It soaked her clothes, stained the earth beneath her.

Haider's stomach lurched. His world spun, the ground beneath him felt unsteady.

He reached out, but it was too late. Darkness closed in.

Haider awoke with a violent jerk, gasping for air. His chest rose and fell in rapid, shallow breaths, his body drenched in sweat. He looked around, disoriented, heart pounding, as if the nightmare had followed him into the real world.

"What happened?" Heidi's voice came from beside him, soft, concerned.

He blinked, his vision blurry. The room was dark, but Heidi was there, sitting on the edge of the bed. Her hand rested gently on his.

"I... I had a nightmare," Haider murmured, his voice hoarse. "I'm... I'm fine. It's just a nightmare."

He held her hand tightly, pressing it against his chest, trying to ground himself. The warmth of her touch was a small comfort, but the sense of dread and something sinister lurking remained. The nightmare was still with him, wrapped around his mind like a vice.

The silence in the room stretched on, but Haider could feel the weight of something just beyond the walls. Something was waiting. The nightmare had only just begun.

Chapter 4

Bound by the Past

The hospital room was quiet, the soft beeping of machines the only sound breaking the heavy silence. Aisha, a woman in her fifties, lay unconscious on the bed, hooked up to an IV drip. The faint scent of antiseptic lingered in the air, mixing with the sterile coldness of the room. Heidi moved quietly beside the bed, her gloved hands gently adjusting the IV line.

The light above flickered briefly, casting long shadows on the walls, but Heidi barely noticed. She was focused on Aisha, her eyes soft but professional as she checked the woman's vital signs.

Suddenly, without warning, Aisha's hand shot out, gripping Heidi's wrist with surprising force. Heidi flinched, startled by the sudden movement. Her eyes widened as Aisha's hand tightened, her fingers digging into Heidi's skin with a strength that didn't seem to match her frail appearance.

"Heidi! Let go! You're hurting her!" Dr. Aliyah's voice called from the doorway, filled with urgency.

Heidi tried to pull away, her wrist straining under Aisha's grip, but the woman's hand remained firmly in place.

Aisha's eyes fluttered open, but they weren't focused—just empty, glazed over, staring at Heidi without recognition.

"Miss Aisha, please," Heidi said, her voice low but trying to remain calm. "You need to let go."

But Aisha's grip didn't loosen. The pressure felt unnatural, like the woman wasn't even aware of what she was doing. Heidi's breathe quickened, but she fought to keep herself composed.

Aliyah moved quickly to Aisha's side, her expression worried as she reached out to help. "Heidi, your wrist... it's bruising. Are you okay?"

"I'm fine," Heidi said quickly, though her voice was strained. She glanced down at her wrist, which was already turning purple. But she pushed past the pain, focusing on Aisha. "I just need to get her to let go."

Her words barely left her mouth when Aisha's body started to tremble, her entire frame shaking as if something was taking control of her. Heidi's heart skipped a beat. She crouched down beside the bed, bringing her face closer to Aisha's, trying to understand what was happening.

Aisha's eyes snapped open, but this time, they were wide and unblinking, filled with a fear that was almost palpable. The woman's lips parted slightly, and in a voice that sounded both strained and distant, she whispered, "You're all evil."

Heidi recoiled as if struck, pulling back quickly from the bed. Aliyah's face shifted with concern. "What does she mean? What's happening to her?"

"I don't know," Heidi muttered, her voice barely above a whisper. She stood frozen for a moment, staring at Aisha's vacant gaze, her mind racing. Something was terribly wrong. This wasn't just a simple medical issue. There was something deeper, darker, happening here.

Aliyah placed a blanket over Aisha and turned to leave the room, her steps quick. "I'll get you a bandage for your wrist."

Heidi stayed behind, her eyes fixed on Aisha as the woman's shallow breathing slowly evened out. She looked almost peaceful now, as though the tension had left her body.

But Heidi couldn't shake the feeling that something had changed. Something was wrong, and Aisha's words echoed in her mind. You're all evil.

Heidi moved quietly down the hall, her steps soundless against the worn tiles. Her movements were fluid, but there was a strange unease about her now, as if her body wasn't fully her own. Her eyes, normally clear and focused, now seemed distant—empty, even. She moved from room to room, checking on her patients with an unsettling detachment.

The air was crisp outside the hospital entrance, the kind of cold that seeped into your bones. Haider stood there, his cigarette dangling between his fingers, the smoke curling lazily upward as if it had all the time in the world. But Haider didn't. His thoughts were elsewhere, trapped in a whirlwind of emotions he didn't know how to process.

The call had come unexpectedly—his father, Faron, after all these years. Haider hadn't even thought about the man in ages. The memories of his father, once so vivid, had faded with time, buried under years of hurt and neglect. He had tried to move on, to forget, but now it seemed the past was coming back to haunt him.

He took a long drag from his cigarette, trying to push away the tension rising in his chest. The ember at the tip glowed brighter as he inhaled deeply, then flicked the cigarette to the ground, crushing it under his boot. The sudden ringing of his phone broke his moment of solitude. He glanced at the screen. An unknown number. His heart skipped a beat.

Without thinking, Haider answered.

"Hello?"

"It's me... your dad," the voice on the other end was calm, collected, almost too calm, as if they were talking about the weather.

Haider froze, his breath caught in his throat. The voice was so familiar, yet so distant, like a ghost from a life he had tried to forget. "How did you get my number?" Haider's voice was a bit more harsh than he intended. His grip tightened on the phone.

"You know who I am. I can get anything I want," Faron's voice carried an eerie confidence, as if he could reach into Haider's life and take whatever he desired, without question. The words made Haider's skin crawl.

"I know that very well. What do you want? Why are you calling?" Haider's pulse quickened, anger mixing with confusion. He hadn't heard from his father in over two decades. What could he possibly want now?

"I miss you," Faron's tone softened in an almost patronizing way. "It's been decades since I saw your face. I want to meet you."

Haider clenched his jaw. The offer of meeting felt hollow. His father's sudden desire to reconnect stirred a deep, unsettling feeling in him. Why now? Why after all this time?

"I can't. I'm busy," Haider's words were clipped, dismissive. But Faron wasn't so easily brushed off.

"I know where you are," he said, his tone growing more persistent. "I'm in town. Come to the house tonight. Have dinner with us."

The invitation hung in the air, heavy with unspoken tension. The thought of returning to that house—the house where so much pain had been inflicted—was nearly too much to bear. But as much as Haider wanted to refuse, something inside him tugged at the thought. Something unresolved.

"Fine," he said, finally, the words tasting bitter on his tongue. "I'll be there."

Later in the evening, the drive to Faron's house was a silent one. Haider's hands gripped the steering wheel tight, knuckles white, his thoughts a tangled mess of past memories and the strange anxiety that gnawed at him.

Beside him, Heidi remained quiet. She could feel the shift in the atmosphere, the unspoken tension hanging between them. It wasn't just about Faron—it was about everything Haider had buried so deep inside. The past he had long since shut away was slowly coming back to life.

Finally, Heidi broke the silence. Her voice was soft, almost cautious, as if testing the waters. "I can't believe you lied to me about your parents' deaths."

Haider's heart skipped a beat at the accusation. It wasn't a lie, not exactly, but it wasn't the whole truth either. He had kept the past buried, hidden away from everyone—including Heidi.

She was the closest person to him now, and yet, there were parts of himself he hadn't shared.

"I didn't lie," Haider said, his voice thick with frustration. He focused on the road, unable to look at her. "My mom died when I was young. After she died, my father... we just became strangers to each other. He never cared, and I didn't care either. Not until yesterday."

Heidi remained silent for a moment, absorbing his words. She could hear the pain beneath the surface, the deep wounds that Haider had never fully healed.

She reached over and placed a hand on his arm, offering him the only comfort she could give in that moment. "You still hate him, don't you?" she asked, her voice gentle but filled with curiosity.

Haider's grip on the steering wheel tightened, his fingers digging into the leather as if it could anchor him to the present, to reality.

His eyes remained fixed on the road, but his thoughts wandered back to the years of neglect, to the harsh words, and the beatings. He didn't have to say it aloud; Heidi could see it in his eyes. The anger, the resentment, still lingered, just beneath the surface.

"Hated," Haider corrected softly, his voice barely above a whisper. "But now... I don't know."

Heidi didn't push him further. She understood that some wounds ran too deep to heal with words. She knew that the past was not something you could just forget. Especially when it was staring you in the face, as it was now.

When they finally arrived at Faron's house, Haider's heart rate quickened. The house loomed before him, a cold, imposing structure that had once felt like home. But now, it felt like a foreign place—a place where he had been a prisoner to his father's cruelty.

Haider hesitated at the door, his hand hovering over the doorbell. His fingers trembled as he reached for it. "Why are your hands shaking?" Heidi asked, her eyes narrowing with concern.

"It's nothing," Haider muttered, but the lie tasted bitter on his tongue. "I just... I can't believe I'm coming back to this place."

Heidi stepped closer, her presence grounding him. "Don't worry," she said, offering him a small, reassuring smile. "Everything will be okay."

But Haider wasn't sure. He couldn't shake the feeling that the past had a way of catching up with you, no matter how hard you tried to escape it.

And this house, these people, were a reminder of all the things he wished he could forget.

The door creaked open, and a woman with warm, welcoming eyes appeared. "Welcome!" she said with a smile that seemed too kind for this house, this place. "I can't believe I'm finally meeting you. By the way, I'm your mom—well, your stepmom! Come in."

Haider didn't know what to say. This woman, Mina, had been married to his father for years now, but she was still a stranger to him. He couldn't bring himself to trust her, to see her as anything more than a symbol of Faron's new life.

Dinner was a quiet, strained affair. Haider, Heidi, Faron, Mina, and Fariya sat at the table, the food delicious but the conversation scarce. The air was thick with unspoken words, and Haider couldn't shake the feeling that he didn't belong here, not anymore.

Faron, trying to break the tension, smiled at Haider. "I wanted you to meet your stepmother and your sister," he said, his voice laced with an odd mixture of pride and arrogance.

Fariya, the young girl, looked at Haider with wide, curious eyes. "Who are they?" she asked innocently, her gaze shifting from Mina to Haider.

Faron smiled indulgently. "This is your older brother, Haider. And this is his wife, Heidi."

Fariya's face lit up, and she turned to Haider with excitement. "I have an older brother? Can you bring me a doll?"

Haider smiled, feeling a rare pang of tenderness. "Of course, I'll bring you the best doll I can find."

The girl rushed over to Haider and kissed him on the cheek, her small hands gripping his arm in a gesture of pure affection. For a moment, Haider almost forgot the bitterness of the past, lost in her innocent joy.

But then, Faron coughed, and the reality of the situation came rushing back. Haider looked at his father, noticing how pale he had become, how weak.

Heidi noticed it too. "Are you okay? You don't look well," she asked, her concern genuine.

Faron waved it off, his voice strained. "I'm fine. Just getting old."

But Heidi wasn't convinced. "You should come to the hospital," she suggested. "It could help."

Faron dismissed her, a faint smile playing at his lips. "I know how to take care of myself."

After dinner, as the night wore on, Heidi pulled Haider aside. "Show me your old room," she said, her voice eager. "I want to see where you grew up."

Haider hesitated.

The thought of revisiting those memories was almost too painful. But Heidi wouldn't take no for an answer.

"Fine," he muttered. "Come on."

Inside his old room, Haider was flooded with memories. The walls were the same, adorned with faded posters and pictures from a life he no longer recognized.

The bed, the desk, the bookshelves—it was all there, just as he had left it. But to him, it was like stepping into a stranger's life.

Heidi looked around, her fingers brushing against the familiar objects as if trying to understand the boy Haider had once been.

Haider swallowed hard, the memories flooding back. "It hasn't changed," he said quietly, his voice distant. "But I have."

Heidi didn't speak. She simply stood by his side, understanding the weight of his words.

As they left the room, Haider couldn't shake the feeling that his past was still clinging to him, pulling him back into the darkness. His father's face, his cold, cruel eyes, haunted him. He didn't know what to expect from this visit, but he knew one thing for certain: the past had never really let him go. And now, it was coming back to collect its due.

Chapter 5

The Father in the Shadows

Heidi's room, bathed in the faint light of the bedside lamp, seemed to close in on Haider, the shadows twisting and shifting as though alive from his past in his mind. The sterile scent of the hospital hung in the air, but it felt suffocating now, more like a tomb than a place of healing.

He swung his legs over the side of the bed and stood up, the cold floor sending a jolt of discomfort through his bare feet. He staggered toward the door, needing to escape, to clear his mind, even if only for a moment.

As his hand reached for the door handle, a sound made him freeze.

The unmistakable, chilling sound of something dripping made Haider's breath catch in his throat as he looked up. The walls outside the room were drenched in blood—fresh blood, still dripping down like crimson rain. He blinked, certain that his mind was playing tricks on him, but the gruesome sight remained.

The hallway stretched out before him, the normally quiet and neutral space now corrupted by violence, the once-white walls now splattered with red. His pulse thundered in his ears, and a cold sweat broke out across his brow.

Then, he saw her.

At the end of the hallway, bathed in the dim, flickering light, stood Heidi. But this wasn't the Heidi he knew. This was something else—something darker, something more sinister.

Her face was pale, her eyes wide and unblinking, her expression twisted with horror and rage. In her hand, she gripped a scalpel, its blade gleaming in the dim light, stained with blood. She is like a predator watching its prey.

Haider's voice faltered as he whispered into the thick silence, "Who are you?"

The words barely left his mouth before Heidi moved. She moved too fast—unnaturally fast—closing the distance between them in the blink of an eye. He stumbled back, heart racing, his throat dry with fear. His body wanted to run, but his legs refused to obey.

Heidi's lips twisted into a cruel, mocking smile, but it wasn't her voice that came from her mouth.

"You know I can kill you," she hissed, in low and guttural man's voice. The voice of something evil.

Haider's breath hitched in his chest, the words catching in his throat. "Do you want to kill me?" he whispered, though the question barely escaped his lips.

For a moment, Heidi's body jerked, as if caught in a violent tug-of-war between two forces. Her grip on the scalpel tightened, but her gaze wavered, as though she was fighting against the darkness that had taken hold of her.

"I'm sorry," Heidi whispers, her voice breaking and raw with emotion. "I didn't mean it. It's not me. It's not me."

But even as she spoke, something changed. The burn marks on her face began to deepen, turning into grotesque, blistering scars.

Her skin seemed to melt away in places, revealing charred, damaged flesh beneath. Haider's stomach churned as he saw the horrifying transformation, his body frozen in place by a paralyzing mixture of fear and helplessness.

"Run, Haider!" Heidi cried, her voice desperate, filled with a terror Haider had never heard before. "Get out of Al Jazab! Get out while you can!"

Tears welled in her eyes, and her hands shook as they reached out, blood dripping from her fingertips. The agony in her eyes was almost too much for Haider to bear, but he couldn't tear himself away.

"I can't leave you, Heidi," he said, his voice thick with emotion. He reached out to take her hand, but her body jerked back in sudden convulsions.

And then, just as quickly as it had begun, Heidi's face contorted in agony, her mouth opening wide in a twisted laugh—one that sent a chill deep into Haider's bones. The sound was not her laugh. It was something darker. Something demonic. Man's laughter.

The oppressive silence of the night hung thick in the air as Haider jolted awake, gasping for breath. His chest heaved his heart racing as his body trembled with the aftermath of a nightmare that felt all too real.

Next morning, Haider awoke with a start, his eyes snapping open to the harsh light of day.

He was back in the hospital, the warmth of the sun streaming in through the window.

The nightmare faded into the back of his mind, though its aftereffects still lingered. His pulse raced in his chest, his body drenched in sweat.

He was exhausted, physically and emotionally drained from the nightmare that had clawed at him throughout the night.

Across the table, Heidi sat, eating her breakfast.

"You look pale," Heidi said, her voice soft and gentle. "Are you alright?"

Haider nodded slowly, rubbing his face with his hand as he tried to shake off the remnants of the dream. He felt disoriented, his body still shaking from the adrenaline that coursed through him.

"I had that nightmare again," Haider muttered, his voice rough. "I don't know how much longer I can take it. Every time I close my eyes, it's like I'm back there."

Heidi's expression softened, and she reached across the table to squeeze his hand. "I know," she said quietly. "I know it's been hard, but we're almost there. Just a few more days, Haider. I promise. And then we can leave. We've done so much good here already."

Haider looked at her, filled with a mix of hope and exhaustion. He wanted to believe her. He wanted to believe that they could leave, that the nightmare would end. But something in the pit of his stomach told him that it wasn't over. Not yet.

KARMA

***

Faron approached the hospital entrance, his steps slow and deliberate. The wind had picked up, causing the trees to sway and the air to feel colder than it should have been for the time of year.

Haider watched him from the window, a sense of unease washing over him. Something about today felt... off. Like the calm before a storm.

Faron's face was drawn, the weight of his years pressing heavily on his shoulders. He had never looked more fragile than he did now, as if the burden of his past was finally catching up to him. Haider didn't know how to feel about his father anymore.

Later that day, Heidi sat beside her father in law, her eyes scanning over the reports, her brow furrowed in concentration. Faron's hands clasped tightly together in his lap, his gaze fixed on the floor. The room felt too quiet, the soft beeping of the machines almost too loud.

"It's good news, Dad," Heidi said softly, breaking the silence.

"Your tests came back fine. You just need to make a few changes to your diet and take your medications regularly. You'll be fine."

Faron looked up at her, his eyes distant, as if the words didn't fully register. For a moment, Heidi thought he might say something, but instead, he just nodded, a noncommittal gesture.

"Take care of yourself, Dad," Heidi said, her voice tinged with concern. "And don't forget to take your medicine."

Faron gave her a weak smile, but it didn't reach his eyes. As he turned to leave, Heidi glanced at the door. For a split second, she thought she saw something—or rather, someone— burnt man standing in the hallway.

Before she could react, the figure disappeared, slipping into the shadows like a phantom.

A cold chill swept over her, and she shivered, her heart pounding in her chest.

As Faron left the room. Heidi stood frozen, the glimpse of burnt man still haunting her mind.

A cold dread settled in her chest, and her thoughts began to twist in a way she couldn't control.

Heidi stormed into her room, slamming the door behind her. The sound echoed through the house, but Haider remained oblivious, his breathing steady as he slept.

Heidi stared at him, a fire burning in her chest, the weight of her thoughts pressing down on her like a vise.

Alone in the bathroom, Heidi slammed her fists onto the sink, the harsh impact reverberating up her arms. Her body shook, her breath ragged.

She stared at her reflection, trying to steady herself. But the voice inside her head—man's voice—was relentless.

"Everything is okay, honey!"

Heidi's jaw clenched. "Should I just kill him?"

The words echoed in her mind, her own voice twisted by the demonic tone man had imbued in her thoughts. She growled the sound barely audible as her fists tightened around the edge of the sink.

She glared into the mirror, her reflection warped by the storm raging inside her. Then, just as her anger reached its peak, burnt man's image appeared in the mirror, his face pale, eyes black as pits.

"You should" he whispered, his voice cold and dark, pulling at her resolve. Heidi's mind was a blur of violent thoughts. She walked back into her room, a strange, creepy smile spreading across her face.

Her fingers curled around the cold metal of the scalpel she held in her hand. She laid down beside Haider, his back turned to her, unaware of the danger so close.

The scalpel gleamed in the dim light as she moved it closer to his throat.

Her heart pounded in her chest, the edge of the blade only inches from his skin. But then, something stopped her—a flicker of hesitation. She froze, her fingers trembling as she hovered above him.

What am I doing? she thought, her mind spiraling. The thought of ending his life was overpowering, yet she couldn't bring herself to do it.

She closed her eyes, letting out a shaky breath, and pulled her hand away. The scalpel clattered quietly on the floor as she sat up, guilt and confusion gnawing at her insides.

Chapter 6

When the Sky Weeps

The sterile, clinical smell of the hospital filled Heidi's nostrils as she stood by the patient counter, her hands gripping a stack of medical forms. Her mind, however, was miles away, trapped in the chaos of her thoughts. The forms blurred before her eyes as her fingers twitched nervously. She wasn't ready, as she wasn't okay.

A faint whisper in her ear, "You're not ready" burnt man's voice murmured. The words crawled under her skin, setting her on edge.

She forced herself to breathe.

The weight of the scalpel in her pocket was a constant reminder of what she was capable of doing. It called to her, beckoning her to use it. She had done it before. The memory of blood on her hands made her stomach churn.

Aliyah stood nearby, watching her with concern.

"Is everything okay?" she asked, her voice laced with worry.

Heidi smiled, though it didn't reach her eyes. "She said, her voice quick, trying to push the darkness back down." "Just need a minute to breathe."

Minutes later, Heidi stood in the operating room, her hands trembling as she stared at the scalpel, feeling its cold weight. She gripped it tighter, her pulse racing in her ears.

She knew what she had to do—she was a surgeon, after all. But something was off. She couldn't stop the rush of panic that washed over her.

The patient lay on the operating table, unaware of the turmoil that raged inside Heidi. She reached toward the injured arm, her fingers itching to fix it, but instead, she scratched at her own body, the sensation grounding her for a moment. The tension inside her rose again.

Aliyah's voice pierced through her haze. "Heidi, are you sure everything's alright?"

Heidi's breath hitched, and for a brief moment, she almost broke. She wanted to scream, to let the chaos inside her explode, but instead, she gave a strained smile.

"Yes," she said again, more firmly this time. "I just need a minute."

***

The evening sun bathed the room in a soft golden glow, though the atmosphere was anything but peaceful. Faron, Mina, and Haider sat together, talking quietly. Fariya played in the corner, her laughter ringing through the room as she held onto a doll Haider had given her. It should have been a warm moment, but something was off.

Haider looked at Faron, his face serious. "She's cute," he said, gesturing toward Fariya. "I really like her, but we're leaving soon. When will you be leaving for the city?"

Faron smiled faintly, but it was a tired, knowing smile. "We'll leave soon, after we sell the house and take care of everything."

Haider's eyes darkened as he spoke again, the words coming out almost cold. "I hope we never meet again," he said, his voice tinged with bitterness.

Faron stiffened. He had known Haider's pain, the loss of his mother still fresh in his mind, but hearing those words hurt more than he expected. Haider continued, his gaze distant.

Haider's voice trembled, but not with sadness—more like a raw wound that had never healed. "You don't understand, Faron. After Mom... after everything, I can't just forget. I don't want to have anything to do with you."

Faron's face tightened, and Mina said nothing, the weight of the silence hanging heavy between them. Haider had made his feelings clear, but that didn't make them any easier to bear.

***

Next day, back in hospital Heidi standing outside, still reflecting about her visits to Fraoon's house. Her mind heavy with thoughts of the long day she had just endured.

KARMA

"Heidi!" Aliyah called, waving an envelope in her hand. Heidi turned, surprised. Aliyah had a bright smile on her face, the kind that always made people feel at ease.

"I wanted to invite you to my wedding," Aliyah said, holding out the card. "It would mean a lot if you could come."

Heidi hesitated for a moment before taking the invitation, nodding with a polite smile. "Thank you, Aliyah. I'll be sure to come."

But as she looked at Aliyah, something felt wrong—an unease prickled at her skin. She couldn't shake the feeling that something dark loomed just beyond the horizon.

The night had fully fallen by the time Aliyah stepped out of the hospital, walking alone down the dimly lit street.

The world around her felt eerily quiet, the only sound the soft click of her footsteps echoing against the pavement.

She was almost home when, from above, a crow fell from the sky, its wings fluttering weakly before its body thudded heavily at her feet. Aliyah stopped in her tracks, her heart skipping a beat.

She knelt down, staring at the lifeless bird, feeling the chill in the air deepen. A strange sense of foreboding washed over her, but she quickly pushed it aside and continued walking, trying to ignore the growing feeling of being watched.

As she passed an alley, a soft moan caught her attention. Aliyah's instincts kicked in, and she rushed toward the sound. In the shadows, she found a woman slumped against the wall, groaning in pain.

Without hesitation, Aliyah helped the woman to her feet. But before she could fully steady the stranger, something wet splashed across her face. She recoiled in shock and horror, her skin burning instantly. The acid seared into her flesh, and she stumbled backward, screaming in pain.

Heidi stood at the end of the alley, a twisted smile on her lips as she watched the woman's skin melt away, disfigured by the corrosive liquid.

The rain began to fall, and Heidi glanced up, her eyes gleaming with something dark and unholy. "It's too early for the sky to start crying," she whispered, her voice shifting into something otherworldly, something not her own.

Aliyah's vision blurred, and she could barely comprehend the words. "Please... don't hurt me! Why are you doing this?" But Heidi didn't answer. Instead, she poured petrol over Aliyah.

"I beg you, don't hurt me," Aliyah cried, her hands shaking as she fell to her knees.

Heidi smiled, her expression cold and detached. "You must die. Everyone must die." She struck the match and tossed it toward her, the fumes thick in the air. With that, Heidi turned and walked away, leaving Aliyah to burn beneath the pouring rain.

Chapter 7

Hell is coming

Back at the hospital, Haider tossed and turned in his bed, disturbed by something he couldn't explain. He woke up suddenly, heart racing, to find that Heidi was not in bed beside him. His thoughts began to spiral. Where had she gone? Had something happened to her?

"Maybe she's checking the patients," Haider muttered, trying to shake the tight grip of fear crawling up his spine.

But as he lay back down, a strange sensation washed over him. The blanket had slowly fallen from his body, now pooled on the floor. The coldness of the room seemed to cling to him, and he shivered despite the warmth of the bed.

His gaze fell to the floor, his eyes widening. There, next to the blanket, was a doll—one he had just given to Fariya.

"I just gave this to Fariya…" he whispered, confused. How had it ended up here?

Haider picked it up, his hand trembling as he moved to the wardrobe. He placed the doll inside and shut the door, but as he did, a soft whisper drifted from within, barely audible, like voices calling to him from the dark. His pulse quickened, and for a moment, his fear was so strong that he couldn't move. Finally, he backed away and ran out of the room, the unease still gnawing at his insides.

Haider stood in the hallway, staring down the dark corridor with wide eyes. Every corner seemed to hold a secret, a presence waiting to strike. He was certain something wasn't right.

He stepped into his room again, eyes scanning the bed. But what he saw made his blood run cold. The blanket, which had been placed neatly on the bed, was now shifting, as if someone—or something—was under it.

His breath caught in his throat as the blanket stirred.

Suddenly, he screamed in terror. But just as quickly, the voice of Heidi rang out behind him.

"What's wrong?" she asked, her voice calm and nonchalant.

"What's wrong?" Haider turned, his breath ragged. Heidi stood there, her expression unreadable, as if nothing was amiss. He spun back to the bed, but there was nothing—just an empty blanket, untouched. No shadow, no presence. Only the silence. "I saw it move," Haider said, his voice barely above a whisper, his chest tight with panic. "I swear something was there."

Heidi stepped forward, her movements slow, almost deliberate, and picked up the blanket. "Were you having a nightmare again?"

"I know what I saw!" Haider insisted, his voice shaking. "This place is haunted. Something's here—something horrible."

Heidi rolled her eyes and sighed. "Don't be ridiculous. It's late, and I'm tired. Let's sleep."

But Haider couldn't. He was convinced that something—or someone—was lurking in the shadows, waiting for the right moment to strike.

As the hours passed and the hospital settled into a tense quiet, Heidi slipped away from the dimly lit hallways. Her footsteps were soft against the sterile floors, a sharp contrast to the muffled sounds of distant conversations. Reaching the stairwell, she ascended without hesitation, her mind clouded with questions. She emerged onto the rooftop, the chill of the night air brushing against her skin. The darkened city stretched before her, a vast, empty expanse. The wind hummed through the silence, carrying whispers that seemed to echo her thoughts. Standing at the edge, she gazed down into the abyss below, her voice a whisper to the void. "What am I supposed to do?" The voice that answered wasn't hers. It was something darker, deeper, and more malevolent.

"Burn them all."

The words were like a punch to the gut, cold and commanding. Her hands clenched into fists, nails biting into her palms. She inhaled sharply, blinking rapidly as if trying to clear her head, but the voice refused to go away.

"No," she muttered under her breath, a tremor in her voice. "I can't..."

For a split second, her gaze wavered, a flicker of doubt crossing her face. But then, her lips pressed together in a hard line. It was too late for doubt now.

She continued to stand there, her body still, but her mind racing, caught between the darkness that whispered to her and the fragments of herself that still fought against it.

Heidi lingered at the entrance of the dimly lit restaurant, her gaze fixed on young man Arslan as he stepped into the night, his hurried pace betraying his eagerness to leave.

Her heart quickened, but not from any concern for him—no, it was something darker, and a pull she couldn't quite explain.

For a moment, she hesitated, standing in the shadows, watching him retreat into the night. The cool air seemed to tighten around her, pressing her, urging her forward. Her fingers twitched at her side, as if the shadows themselves were calling her to follow.

Without another thought, she moved, her high heels clicking sharply on the empty street. The sound reverberated through the stillness, the rhythm of her steps echoing louder than her thoughts, almost as if the night itself was holding its breath.

The flickering streetlights cast an eerie glow on the scene as they walked. Heidi's white dress fluttered in the breeze, her long hair swaying with every step she took. There was something unsettling about the way she moved—almost as if she wasn't truly alive. Her eyes were fixed on Arslan, a predator stalking its prey.

Suddenly, Arslan turned around. For a brief moment, his gaze met hers, and he froze. What he saw made his blood run cold. Heidi's face had an unnatural stillness to it.

She reached into her purse, her fingers brushing against the cold steel of a scalpel. With a swift motion, she pulled it out. Arslan's heart raced as he turned to run.

But it was too late.

His foot caught on something, and he stumbled, crashing to the ground. Before he could get back up, Heidi was there. The possessed woman grabbed him by the throat with an inhuman strength. The last thing Arslan felt was the cold, sharp blade of the scalpel slashing across his throat.

Faron was sound asleep when his phone buzzed, jolting him awake. The screen lit up with a chilling message: *Hell is coming*. He rubbed his eyes, confused, before pressing play on the video attached to the message. What he saw made his stomach churn. The lifeless body of Arslan, his throat gruesomely slit, lay sprawled across the floor. Blood pooled beneath him, and the horror of it seeped into Faron's very bones.

The video ended. Faron stared at the screen, a sickened dread creeping over him. His heart pounded, but his mind couldn't fully process what he had just seen.

***

The morning sunlight filtered through the curtains, but it didn't ease the tension in Faron's mind. He sat at the table, staring blankly at his breakfast. His mind was still trapped in the horrific images of the video. Mina and Fariya sat across from him, but their presence barely registered.

Mina noticed the far-off look in his eyes and frowned. "What's wrong? You look sick."

Faron blinked, as if coming out of a trance. He gave her a forced smile. "Don't worry, I'm fine."

Faron stepped out of the house, a quiet goodbye to Mina on his lips. He didn't notice how his steps seemed heavier than usual until, suddenly, he lost his footing. The ground beneath him seemed to tilt, and he tumbled down the steps.

"Mina!" he called out, trying to push himself up, but his legs wouldn't cooperate. Pain shot through him, and he fell back onto the ground, grimacing.

Mina rushed to his side, concern written all over her face. "Are you okay?"

"I'm fine," Faron muttered, though the words didn't convince either of them.

Later in hospital, Mina, Haider stood beside Faron, watching Heidi examine his swollen feet. Heidi's hands moved with practiced care as she reassured him. "It's nothing to worry about, Dad. But you need to rest. No physical activity for a few days."

Before Faron could respond, Jazmin entered the room, holding a tray of medicine. But as soon as she saw Faron, her face twisted with fury. The tray trembled in her hands, and she dropped it, her eyes locking onto Faron with an expression that bordered on madness.

Mina's heart skipped a beat. She saw something she couldn't explain—the burnt figure of a man stood behind Heidi, his form flickering like a ghost in her vision. She retrograde and start running.

Mina's legs felt heavier than ever, as if the weight of her fear had become a physical force, pulling her down with every step. Her thoughts were tangled, no longer her own. The vision of burned man haunted her mind and the cold walls of the hospital offered no escape.

The hallway stretched on, a maze of flickering lights and dark corners. But then, she saw it—an acid bottle sitting on a nurse's cart, just a few steps away.

It felt like it was calling to her, a lifeline or a trap. Her hand trembled as it closed around the bottle, the glass cold against her fingers.

The urge to do something—anything—was suffocating.

She stared at the bottle, her breath shallow, and for a second, she hesitated.

"No," she whispered. "I can't."

But then, burnt man's ghost appeared again, a flicker in the corner of her eye. His hollow eyes, his charred face—his presence consumed her. It was like his voice was inside her head. "You can't escape," it seemed to whisper.

Some external power forces her to grab the bottle. With a shaky gasp, she gripped the bottle tightly. Her body was moving before she even realized it, her hand lifting the bottle high, shaking with fear and confusion.

She felt the weight of her own soul slipping away, as if the bottle wasn't hers to control anymore. The acid splashed onto her skin with a hiss. A scream tore from her throat, raw and anguished. The world spun as the pain hit her like a firestorm, her flesh burning, bubbling, and disintegrating. Every movement only worsened the agony.

She stumbled backward, vision swimming. Her hands reached to wipe the acid from her face, but it only intensified the pain, peeling her skin away with each touch.

"Haider..." The whisper escaped her lips, a faint plea for help that seemed lost in the suffocating haze.

Haider's voice cut through the fog. "Mina!" His voice was frantic, desperate—he was there, but the world felt too far away.

She felt his arms around her, pulling her into his chest. She was weightless, her body limp, and the world blurred into a chaotic whirlwind of pain and confusion.

Haider's hands shook as he wrapped her in a blanket, his face pale with terror. "I've got you. You're going to be okay."

Panic clawed at him as he lifted her, fear twisting his chest. The hospital hallways felt like miles as he rushed toward the ICU, his steps heavy, heart pounding.

Chapter 8

Descent into Hell

Outside the small ward, Faron and Haider stood in the dim hallway, tension heavy between them. Faron's face was tight with worry, his eyes dark with a fear that Haider couldn't quite understand. They stood there, silent for a moment, when Jazmin suddenly appeared, her hands shaking with fury.

"You devil!" she screamed at Faron, her voice sharp and full of grief. "You killed my son and daughter-in-law!"

Faron pushed her away, frustration in his eyes. "Get off me, old lady! Are you crazy?" he snapped.

Haider stepped in; trying to calm the situation, but Jazmin was too far gone, her grief overwhelming her.

"Are you okay?" he asked her softly, but his concern quickly turned to anger when he saw how Faron was acting. "What's wrong with you, Dad?"

"She attacked me!" Faron barked, his voice trembling with a mix of anger and fear.

Nurses arrived and quickly took Jazmin away, but not before she screamed again, "My poor Amir! You devil, you killed my son! You all deserve to die! You will all die!"

The words hung in the air, a chilling prediction of what was to come.

***

Haider sat on a bench outside the ward, his face tense, his mind racing. He could feel the weight of the questions pressing on him, and he couldn't shake the feeling that something was deeply wrong. His thoughts were interrupted when Faron approached, his voice low and urgent.

"I need to talk to you about something," Faron said, his gaze flicking nervously to the door of the ward.

Haider looked up, his eyes narrowing. "Okay, I'm listening."

"I think you and Heidi should go back to the city," Faron said, his tone final, as if the decision had already been made.

Haider shook his head. "Why? What are you talking about?"

"With everything that's happening around here, I don't think it's the right place for you and Heidi anymore," Faron insisted, his voice almost pleading.

"No," Haider said, his voice firm. "I'm not leaving you here by yourself. No matter what happened between us, we're family. We're staying until Mina gets better."

Faron's expression hardened. "This is not a suggestion. I'm telling you to go back."

Haider stood, his fists clenched. "Why? What are you hiding from me?"

"Because I'm saying so!" Faron snapped, his voice rising with frustration.

Haider's eyes flashed with suspicion. "What are you not telling me, Dad?"

"You saw what happened to Mina, right?" Faron said, his voice barely a whisper. "There's something going on here. Something you don't understand."

Haider's gaze hardened. "Yes, I saw it. There must be some kind of medical explanation, right?"

Faron's face twisted in frustration. "Please, just listen to me! This isn't the place for you."

Haider shook his head, disbelief spreading across his face. "Who is Amir?" he asked, his voice low and demanding.

Faron hesitated, his eyes shifting nervously. "I don't know," he said, but the lie was clear.

"You're lying!" Haider shouted. "Tell me the truth! Why did that old nurse say you killed him?"

"That old nurse is crazy!" Faron barked. "She should be in a mental hospital or in jail!"

***

Heidi dragged Mina toward the window, her grip tightening with each step.

The small ward seemed to hold its breath, the sterile air thick with the tension between them.

Outside Haider and Faron heard a noise and rushed inside the ward, unaware of the unfolding danger.

Mina teetered on the edge of the window, her body swaying as she struggled against Heidi's force. Behind her, Heidi stood like a shadow, her eyes cold with determination. Haider limped into the room, Faron at his side.

Heidi shoved Mina from the window. The sickening thud of her body hitting the ground echoed in Haider's mind as his heart lurched.

"No!" Haider shouted. "Heidi! What have you done?"

Heidi turned, her expression contorting into something monstrous. She stepped toward Haider with a deliberate pace, her hands shooting out to grip his neck. Her voice, when she spoke, was not her own—it was a guttural, distorted growl, like something possessed.

"It's all your father's fault," Heidi snarled, her words thick with venom. "How dare he touch my mom?"

With a sudden and brutal shove, Heidi pushed Haider out through the door, sending him crashing into the yard. His body lay still, unconscious.

Heidi turned her cold gaze toward Faron. Fear flashed in his eyes as he stumbled backward, crawling away from the advancing threat.

Heidi moved toward him slowly, almost casually, the predatory look in her eyes unyielding.

Haider regained consciousness with a sharp gasp, his head pounding. Slowly, he rose to his feet, disoriented but driven by a single purpose: find Heidi and Faron.

The hospital's sterile hallways felt endless as Haider searched every room, calling their names. But they were nowhere to be found. A sense of dread gnawed at his insides, pushing him to act faster.

Haider's anxiety escalated as he reached Faron's house. His knuckles rapped sharply against the door, his mind racing. When the door swung open, it revealed Faroon's housekeeper Shazia, her expression drawn with worry.

"Is my father here?" Haider asked, his voice tight with urgency.

"No," Shazia replied, shaking her head. "They're not here. They went to the hospital and haven't come back yet."

Haider's brow furrowed, a sense of unease settling over him. "Where's Fariya?"

"She's playing in her room."

Haider nodded absently, already turning to leave, but then he paused, his eyes locking with Shazia's. "Be alert," he warned. "Don't open the door for any strangers."

Without waiting for a response, he walked briskly away, the weight of his worry heavy in his chest.

Haider pushed through the hospital doors and entered the nurse station, his eyes scanning the room in search of Jazmin.

His chest tightened with each passing second, and he couldn't shake the feeling that something was off. She wasn't in sight.

His gaze flickered toward the counter, where nurse was sitting, absorbed in her work. Haider strode over, his footsteps echoing through the sterile hallway.

"Do you know where Jazmin is?" he asked, trying to keep his voice steady despite the rising unease in his chest.

Nurse glanced up, her face calm but tired. She hesitated, as if unsure whether to speak. "She was under a lot of stress," the lady explained, her tone softening with sympathy. "The management sent her on medical leave."

Haider's eyes narrowed, his frustration surfacing. "She attacked my father," he snapped. "How can you just let her go?"

Nurse's expression faltered, but she didn't answer right away. After a tense moment, she reached for a small piece of paper and scribbled something on it before handing it over. "This is her address," she said quietly. "I'm not sure where she's staying now, but... this is where she was last."

Haider took the paper without a word, his mind racing. He turned and left the nurse station, the feeling of unease growing heavier with each step.

***

Haider stood in front of Jazmin's house, his pulse quickening as the silence of the street pressed in around him. The air felt heavy, like something was about to shift, but he couldn't place what it was.

His hand hovered over the doorbell, the cold metal button feeling like a weight in his palm.

He took a deep breath, his mind racing with the strange memories of the last few days at the hospital, Mina's unsettling behavior, Faron's cryptic warnings.

Each moment had led him here, to this doorstep, but the pieces weren't fitting.

"Was it a mistake to come?" he wondered, his instincts screaming at him to turn back.

Jazmin's words still echoed in his mind, haunting him. "You killed my son…" But how could that be? His father… Mina… none of this made sense.

With a resigned breath, he pressed the button, and the door creaked open, revealing Jazmin standing in the doorway.

Her face was unreadable, distant—like she was waiting for something, or perhaps expecting someone, but there was no warmth in her greeting.

"How are you feeling now?" Haider asked, trying to mask the fear in his voice with concern.

Jazmin didn't reply. She merely stepped aside, an almost imperceptible gesture that allowed him to enter.

He hesitated but stepped in, immediately sensing something was off. The house felt too quiet, too still, as though time itself had slowed down.

His eyes scanned the room, eventually falling on a photograph on a nearby table.

The photograph was simple, yet it felt like a weight on his chest. In the picture, the family stood together, their smiles frozen in time, but it was the girl that held his attention. Her eyes bright and full of life. Haider's breath caught in his throat as his gaze locked onto her face. She was the same girl from his nightmares. "Who are they?" he asked, his voice hesitant, trying to keep his composure.

At the mention of Amir's name, a brief flicker of something dark flashed in Jazmin's eyes, an unsettling change in her expression that only Haider seemed to notice. Then, in the blink of an eye, her lips curled into a twisted smile—one that didn't quite belong on her face.

It was too wide, too eerie, as though she were a different person altogether.

"Would you like some tea?" she asked, her tone syrupy sweet, as if nothing was amiss.

A cold shiver ran down Haider's spine. His instincts screamed at him to turn and leave, but his body moved before his mind could catch up. His hands shook slightly as he wiped his forehead, sweat beading as the oppressive silence of the room pressed in on him.

Jazmin turned and walked toward the kitchen, her movements unnervingly calm.

Haider stood there, trying to steady his breathing, but it was impossible. Every instinct he had told him that something was terribly wrong.

She returned a few moments later, carrying a steaming cup of tea. She placed it in front of him with deliberate care, her gaze never leaving him.

"I think you have questions," Jazmin said, her voice a little too smooth, a little too knowing. "Ask away."

Haider stared at the tea, the steam rising from it in delicate swirls, but he could hardly bring himself to take a sip.

His mind raced as he tried to gather his thoughts. This was the moment he had been waiting for—the truth, the answers. The questions burned in his chest.

Taking a steadying breath, he finally lifted the cup to his lips and drank, the warmth doing little to ease the storm inside him. He set it down slowly.

"What happened to your son?" he asked, his voice shaking slightly.

"How did he die? And what does his death have to do with my father? Why does he possess my wife?"

The room seemed to grow colder as he finished, the weight of his words hanging in the air.

Jazmin didn't answer immediately. Instead, she locked her gaze onto him, her eyes never leaving his. It was as if she were savoring his discomfort, drawing out the moment for some private, sadistic pleasure.

And then, everything went dark.

Haider's senses returned to him in fragments. His head throbbed painfully, and the world around him felt distorted, like he was seeing everything through a fog. Slowly, the realization set in. His wrists were bound tightly, the ropes digging into his skin.

He couldn't move. Panic surged through him, suffocating him with its intensity. His heart raced, and his throat constricted, but he couldn't make a sound.

Jazmin stood before him now, her face cold and distant.

"Why do you want to kill my father?" he managed to choke out. "Where is my father? Where is my wife?"

Jazmin's eyes widened with a hint of something almost... satisfied. She leaned closer, her breath hot against his ear.

"Do you want to know the truth?" she asked, her voice low and predatory.

Before Haider could react, she placed a strip of tape over his mouth, silencing him. Her voice dropped to a whisper, her breath sending a shiver through his entire body.

"You father deserve to die..." she hissed, her words sharp like a blade. "To burn alive and go to hell. Do you know why?"

Haider's heart stopped in his chest. The terror gripped him in ways he couldn't explain. Her words echoed in his ears, haunting him. And yet, he could do nothing but listen, paralyzed by fear.

Chapter 9

A Hell of a Misunderstanding

Flashback: The sun casts a soft golden light over the peaceful pond. A gentle breeze ripples the water's surface, and delicate butterflies flutter through the air, their wings shimmering in the sunlight. The air smells of fresh earth and flowers, a tranquil moment frozen in time.

A little girl, around six years old, runs barefoot along the edge of the pond, her laughter mingling with the sounds of nature. Her name is Amina.

She wears a simple, light dress, and her dark hair bounces with each playful step. The world is her playground, full of wonder and innocence.

Amina stops suddenly, kneeling by a large stone near the water. She picks it up with both hands, her small fingers gripping the rough surface.

Beneath it, hidden among the dirt and leaves, lies a rusty nail. It gleams in the sunlight, sharp and forgotten. As she lifts the stone, her finger brushes the nail, and a sharp sting shoots through her hand.

She looks down at her finger, surprised to see a thin stream of blood trickling from the small cut. But her expression is fleeting. Without a word, she simply watches the red liquid gather before it slowly drips onto the ground.

Amina winces, but only for a moment. With a small shake of her head, she lets out a soft laugh, brushing off the pain. She continues playing, her attention shifting back to the butterflies fluttering nearby. Her small hand remains covered in the faint trace of blood, but it doesn't stop her. She is lost in her world of carefree joy, unbothered by the injury.

***

The family sat together at the dinner table, the soft clinking of cutlery filling the room. Amir, a man in his forties, and Samira, his wife in her mid-thirties, sat across from Amina. The food was simple, yet lovingly prepared, a steaming bowl of sweet rice that Samira had cooked herself.

Suddenly, Amina's spoon slipped from her hand and clattered to the floor.

"What's wrong, Amina?" Samira asked, her voice filled with concern as she looked at her daughter.

Amir, who had already risen from his seat, picked up the spoon and handed it to Samira. She wiped it clean with a cloth before offering it back to Amina.

"Go ahead. Eat," Samira said with a soft smile, urging her daughter to continue.

But Amina hesitated. Her small hand shook slightly as she took the spoon, and then set it down again without eating. Samira's concern grew.

"What's wrong? It's good. I cooked sweet rice for you. Eat. Open your mouth. Ahh!" Samira encouraged, trying to feed Amina.

Amir, watching this exchange, interrupted gently but firmly.

"You're pampering her too much," he said, his tone a little sharp. "Let her eat by herself."

Samira frowned, brushing a stray lock of hair behind her ear. "Amina has a slight cold."

"She should still eat more," Amir replied, his voice a little more forceful now.

Samira sighed. "She couldn't even open her mouth at the hospital yesterday. The doctor seemed annoyed with her."

Amir's eyes narrowed slightly, as if questioning the seriousness of the situation.

"Didn't the doctor examine her carefully?" he asked, looking at Amina, who seemed to shrink into herself.

"Now, Amina. Eat. Open your mouth. Amina, eat!" Amir insisted.

Reluctantly, Amina opened her mouth and started eating, but her movements were slow and hesitant.

Later that night, Samira sat beside Amir in their bedroom, holding a doll that Amina had once played with in her younger years. She sighed deeply, a wave of sadness crossing her face.

"Poor child. She doesn't even have a nice toy," Samira murmured. "And you're too hard on her. She's become depressed. She just started kindergarten, for heaven's sake.

She's so small—only a fraction of your size. To her, you must seem like a master. Amina can't endure that way... You keep ordering her around."

Amir listened in silence, guilt creeping into his expression. His heart softened, but he still felt a certain tension, unsure how to approach the situation.

Amir stepped quietly into Amina's room, where his daughter lay sleeping. The soft rise and fall of her small chest filled the room with a quiet peace, but Amir couldn't shake the feeling of unease that gripped him. His eyes lingered on her face—pity and love in equal measure.

The next day, Samira walked through the neighborhood, grocery bags in her hands, and a new doll tucked under her arm for Amina. She entered the house with a soft sigh, her heart heavy with concern.

Amir took Amina's hand gently, leading her toward her room. "Come, look," he said, his voice tender yet strained.

Amina stumbled as she walked, and suddenly she fell to the ground with a cry of pain. Samira rushed to her side, her face filled with worry.

"What's wrong?" Samira asked, kneeling beside her daughter. "Why are you walking strangely? Are you hurt?"

Amina shook her head, but the tears in her eyes betrayed her discomfort.

"I'm alright," she muttered, trying to push herself up.

Amir, standing nearby, eyed his daughter with growing concern. "Then you should be able to walk normally. Try again."

"I can, but I don't want to," Amina said quietly.

Samira, watching this interaction with growing fear, turned to Amir. "I hope it's not polio," she whispered. "Is it?"

Amir's expression hardened. "Silly! Don't say things like that."

He looked at Amina again, his eyes narrowing with worry. "What did the doctor say?

Samira's frustration bubbled over. "She didn't examine her properly," she said, her voice tinged with anger. "She didn't take us seriously."

"I'll go to a different doctor tomorrow," Amir promised, his voice cold.

"Please do," Samira pleaded, her voice trembling with the strain of the situation.

Amina lay in bed, seemingly lost in a deep, restless sleep.

Amir and Samira lay together, the weight of the day's events pressing down on them. Amir finally spoke, his voice heavy with regret.

"You were right. I've been too harsh on her. I'll try to be a better father."

Suddenly, they heard a scream. It was Amina's voice—sharp, filled with terror.

Without a word, both Amir and Samira rushed toward Amina's room. The door was slightly ajar, and as they pushed it open, they found Amina standing by her bed, her body stiff, her face pale and confused.

"What happened?" Samira cried, rushing to her daughter's side. Amina's neck had become rigid, and her eyes darted around, unfocused.

Amir's face went pale with fear. Amina's body began to tremble, and before they could react, she collapsed to the floor, her limbs jerking uncontrollably. "Call an ambulance!" he screamed at Samira.

Samira immediately dialed the phone, her voice trembling as she spoke to the operator. "Send an ambulance! My daughter collapsed!"

Amir sprinted toward the ambulance, his arms wrapped around Amina's small body. Samira followed, her face etched with terror. They were running out of time.

Inside the sterile hospital room Amir sat beside doctor Aliyah.

Doctor's face was grim as she spoke, her words sending a chill through the air. "You better send her to a bigger hospital."

"What's wrong with her?" Amir asked, his voice hoarse.

"It seems something is wrong with her brain," Aliyah replied.

Amir's heart skipped a beat. "You mean encephalitis? Or something else?"

Aliyah shook her head. "I don't know yet."

"You said it was just a cold yesterday!" Samira cried, her voice filled with disbelief.

Amir turned to Aliyah, his voice hardening. "Is it alright if we leave her here tonight and go to the big hospital in the morning?"

"I'm afraid it won't make a difference. Take her home," Aliyah said, her tone flat.

Samira sat outside the hospital, cradling Amina in her lap, her heart heavy with worry. Amir was still trying to hail a taxi, but none would stop.

"They won't even take care of her for one night!" Samira snapped, her frustration boiling over.

Amir kept his focus, trying to stay calm. "Don't blame the doctor. I'm sure she has a reason for what she said."

"Your own child is in trouble, and you're so generous!" Samira retorted. "How can you be so calm?"

Samira's tears began to flow, her voice breaking. "I'm not going to let anything happen to my daughter."

Desperate, Samira stood up and waved her arm, trying to stop taxi. Still, no taxis stopped.

The night felt suffocating, a constant reminder of how fragile life could be. The cold night air did nothing to numb the crushing weight of helplessness that hung between them. Samira's sobs echoed through the empty street, but it felt like no one was listening.

No one was coming to help. She wanted to scream, to tear apart the injustice that had been dealt to them, but her voice failed her.

Amir glanced up just as a taxi finally approached. He stood up in a daze, unable to fully process the sight of it. "We need to get her to the hospital," he said.

Samira goes inside the taxi while holding Amina, her heart pounding.

The taxi screeched to a halt outside the imposing doors of the hospital, its bright lights cutting through the darkness. Amir and Samira scrambled out of taxi, still holding Amina's lifeless body between them, fear gripping their every move. Their breaths came in frantic gasps as they rushed inside, their shoes slapping against the cold, sterile floor.

Samira's eyes were wide with terror, her voice breaking as she called out to the nurses. "Please! My daughter! Help her!" Her plea echoed through the busy emergency room, but no one seemed to react fast enough. Amir pushed forward, his eyes frantic, but the nurses simply pointed to a nearby desk where they could register their daughter.

"Register her first!" a nurse called out, the sharpness in her voice pulling Samira back to reality.

"Please, she's not breathing!" Amir's voice cracked as he yelled at them. The urgency in his tone finally caught their attention.

Within moments, a team of doctors and nurses surrounded them, pushing Samira and Amir aside as they worked quickly to assess Amina's condition. Their hands were steady and practiced, but Samira could see the doubt in their eyes. It was too late. The fight had been lost long before they had arrived.

"Clear!" one of the doctors said, applying the defibrillator to Amina's small chest. The machine hummed, a sharp electric pulse racing through her tiny body. Samira's heart stopped with each failed attempt to revive her daughter.

"Again! Again!" Amir shouted, his voice breaking as he pleaded for them to do more. But the doctors exchanged looks—brief, solemn, and understanding. One of them, a man with kind eyes, took a step closer to Amir.

"I'm sorry," he said quietly. "There's nothing more we can do. She's gone."

Samira's world shattered. The walls of the hospital blurred as she crumbled to the floor, her body shaking uncontrollably. She couldn't process the words. She couldn't understand. How could this be real? How could her daughter, her precious Amina, be gone?

"No… no, no, no…" Samira's voice was a broken whisper as she reached out for her daughter, her arms empty as the reality set in. Amir stood frozen, his face pale, his breath shallow, as if the very air had been stolen from him.

The doctor gave them a moment—just a moment—before gently placing a hand on Samira's shoulder. "I'm so sorry for your loss."

***

Few months later, news of the recent disappearances spread through the town. Police officers were investigating the bodies of children—four, eight, and fourteen years old. The signs of their organs being removed were chilling.

***

Faron with his family knocked on Amir's door.

"Come in," Amir said, gesturing inside.

Inside, Amir led Faron and Mina through the house, showing them around.

When they came to the kitchen, Fariya ran outside to play. Amir's eyes followed her for a moment before he turned back to Mina.

"Can I ask how old she is?" Amir said, his voice soft.

"She's six," Mina replied, her voice gentle.

"So she's in kindergarten," Amir observed.

"Yes," Mina replied.

"Amina was the same age when she... when she died," Amir said.

Faron glanced at Amir, his brow furrowing in confusion.

"What happened to her?" Faron asked, his voice hard.

"She died recently," Amir replied quietly. "My wife is unwell too, and that's why we're thinking about selling the house."

Fariya, meanwhile, had wandered outside and, distracted, fell to the ground, scraping her knees. She began to cry, blood dripping from her wounds. Samira holding grocery bags, rushed to her side, kneeling to comfort the child.

"Are you hurt? Why are you crying?" Samira asked, lifting the girl into her arms.

"Stop crying," Samira said softly. "Do you want some candy?"

The rain began to fall, and Samira wrapped her long scarf around Fariya to protect her from the cold.

Back inside, Faron and Mina searched for Fariya. Amir noticed the absence of the girl and furrowed his brow.

"She's probably outside," he said, standing up.

Faron, Mina, and Amir searched outside for Fariya. As they walked, they saw Samira walking toward them, holding Fariya in her arms.

Faron's expression darkened.

"Who the hell are you?" Faron demanded. "Where are you taking my daughter?"

Before Samira could respond, Faron saw the blood on Fariya's knees. In a moment of rage, he slapped Samira hard across the face.

Amir, now beside Samira, pushed Faron away with all his strength.

"How dare you hit my wife?" Amir shouted, his voice shaking with fury.

Faron's face twisted in anger. "So you're in this together. You lost your own daughter and now you're trying to steal mine."

Amir's voice trembled with shock and disbelief. "What the hell are you talking about?"

Without warning, Faron struck Amir across the face, knocking him back. He grabbed Amir by the collar, lifting him up.

"Trying to act innocent?" Faron spat. "You both are caught red-handed. I know what you're trying to do."

The confrontation escalated quickly, and Faron pulled out his phone to call the police.

The tension in the room was suffocating. Faron's face was twisted in anger as he stood across from Mina, Samira, Amir, and Owais (police officer). The walls of the police station seemed to close in on them as the argument escalated.

"I want them to be hanged," Mina's voice rang out, sharp and full of conviction.

Faron shook his head, his fists clenched at his sides. "No! They should be burned alive! Let them feel the pain they've caused."

Samira's voice cracked as she tried to intervene. "No... no, sir, it's all just a misunderstanding. She fell down, and I was just trying to console her." Her words were desperate, pleading, but they fell on deaf ears.

Owais stood beside her, listening with furrowed brows as Samira and Amir tried to explain. But Faron wasn't listening. His eyes narrowed, and he seemed to be lost in his own rage. Meanwhile, Faron's phone buzzed in his pocket.

With a quick glance at the screen, Faron's lips curled into a knowing smile. He pulled the phone from his pocket and quickly typed a message.

FARON'S PHONE: *Come to the police station. Bring as many people as possible.*

He hit send without hesitation.

Outside, the street was filling with people. At first, it was a few, then dozens, and soon, a crowd had gathered at the entrance to the station.

They stood, waiting for something — anything — to happen. The air was thick with whispers, rumors circulating like wildfire. Phones glowed as people checked their messages, eager to be a part of whatever was unfolding inside.

Faron's phone buzzed again. He glanced at the message.

FARON'S PHONE: *We are here.*

He didn't waste a second before responding.

FARON'S PHONE: *Come inside.*

And then, the doors of the station burst open. Arslan and his followers stormed in, their voices loud, their anger palpable. The air grew thick with their fury as they shouted in unison, feeding off each other's rage. The chaos had only just begun.

Faron seized the moment. He grabbed Amir by the collar and dragged him outside, throwing punches as he went. Amir struggled, his hands bound and weak, but Faron was relentless. The crowd followed, their voices growing louder with each step.

Outside, the situation was quickly spiraling out of control. Owais tries to push through the throngs of people to stop Faron, but it was impossible. The crowd surged forward, pushing them aside, their eyes wild with the same fury that had overtaken Faron.

Owais stood, helpless, shouting for calm. "They are not child abductors! It's all a misunderstanding!" His voice cracked with desperation, but the words barely reached the ears of the crowd. His pleas were drowned out by the rising anger.

People were holding their phones aloft, capturing every moment. The message spread quickly through the crowd.

The rumor was spreading, growing, gaining power with every passing second.

PHONE SCREENS: *"Child kidnappers have been caught. Come to the police station."*

Arslan's voice cut through the noise, his words ringing out like a rallying cry. "It appears that these criminals are involved in organ trafficking..." His eyes glinted with excitement as he spoke into his phone, live-streaming the chaos. "In the past few days, children aged four, eight and fourteen have disappeared. A couple of them have been found dead, their organs removed."

Arslan nodded solemnly at the camera, his face a mask of righteous anger. "Believe me, the kidnappers are here," he said, his voice full of conviction, though the truth seemed lost in the madness.

The crowd responded with fury, a chant rising from the chaos. They were ready to see blood, ready to exact their revenge, no matter the cost.

Samira and Amir were still struggling, pushed to the ground as Faron stood above them, his eyes wild with rage. He reached into a canister of petrol, pouring it over both of them. Samira lay motionless, her eyes closed, her body limp. But Amir still breathed, albeit weakly, his chest rising and falling slowly.

The crowd stood in silence for a moment, as if waiting, unsure. Then, Faron struck a match, and the flames ignited.

The fire roared to life, engulfing Samira and Amir in an instant. The crackling of the flames drowned out the screams, the heat searing through the air.

The crowd cheered, their faces illuminated by the flames, their phones raised high to capture the moment. But as the smoke began to rise, the faces in the crowd shifted from elation to uncertainty.

Amir's limbs twitched, struggling against the inevitable, but it was too late. The flames consumed them both, and soon the columns of smoke were visible from every corner of the town.

The sky was a pale gray, the clouds heavy, as if the heavens themselves mourned the loss. A crowd of people gathered around the grave, their heads bowed in silence. Among them stood Jazmin, distant and isolated from the others.

Tears blurred her vision, but she didn't try to wipe them away. Grief tore through her with each passing second. Her chest tightened as her sobs came, quiet at first, but soon uncontrollable. Jazmin couldn't breathe without feeling the absence of her son and daughter—their laughter, their joy, their futures ripped away in an instant.

She stood motionless, her heart breaking with every breath.

Chapter 10

Vengeance from Hell

The room was dim, shadows cast by the low light, adding to the oppressive atmosphere. Haider sat in a chair, his body tied tightly with coarse rope, his head hanging low. He was bruised, his face pale with exhaustion, but his eyes—those eyes—still held a fierce spark of defiance.

Jazmin was opposite him, her posture rigid, her hands still clutching the things belong to her son and daughter in law. The items seemed to burn through her, a constant reminder of what had been stolen from her.

She stood there for a long moment, her chest heaving as she fought to calm the raging storm inside her. The silence between them was thick, almost suffocating, as the anger and sorrow within her swirled together. She opened her mouth, her voice trembling as the words escaped her lips.

"This is what your father did to my family," she whispered, the pain raw and heavy in her tone. But then the words began to build, the quiet grief turning into something darker, something more dangerous. "My son... my daughter... they were good people! They didn't deserve what happened to them. They didn't deserve this!"

The words cracked as they left her throat, her voice rising in a desperate, angry shout. She stepped forward, the trembling in her hands now a reflection of the fury burning inside her.

"You'll all pay!" she shouted, her eyes fierce as they locked onto Haider's. "For what your father did. You will pay for all of it. For the lives he took. You will pay for his sins."

***

At Amir's house, Heidi's grip tightened around Faron's neck, her fingers like iron bands. Her eyes glowed with a terrifying, unnatural light. With one fluid motion, she lifted him off the ground, her strength unnatural, beyond human. Her voice, when it came, was no longer hers. It was deep, guttural—laced with a demonic power.

"We now finally end our ill-fated relationship," Heidi's voice rasped, echoing with the twisted undertones of Amir's spirit. "At the place from where it all started."

With a violent shove, Heidi threw Faron to the ground. He hit the floor with a sickening thud, gasping for breath, his body aching. Panic surged through him as he scrambled to his feet, his muscles protesting the strain, and crawled toward the next room, desperate to escape the nightmare unfolding.

But Heidi was relentless. She stepped forward, smiling with twisted glee, and her presence seemed to suck the very air from the room.

"Please, I'm sorry for everything," Faron whispered, crawling, desperate to save his life, but Heidi's laugh echoed coldly in response.

She moved swiftly, too swiftly. Before Faron could react, Heidi grabbed him again, dragging him back to the center of the room. Her hands were everywhere—tying him, binding him to the floor with rough, unyielding rope.

"I'm not going to let you get away that easily," she murmured, her voice still thick with Amir's demonic echo, a dark promise.

Faron's body was trapped, his limbs painfully bound. Fear gripped him as he struggled against the ropes, his chest rising and falling with quick, shallow breaths.

"Let me go!" he shouted, his voice raw, desperate. His eyes darted around the room, searching for a way to escape, but there was nothing. The walls felt as if they were closing in on him.

Heidi didn't respond immediately. Instead, she moved to the table, her movements deliberate and cold. She picked up a small candle, its wax smooth and untouched, and a matchbox.

The sound of the match striking against the box filled the silence, a sharp, sickening sound. She lit the candle, the flame dancing in the dark, casting eerie shadows across her face.

"No! Let me go!" Faron screamed, his voice breaking as the terror surged within him. He could feel the heat of the flame from across the room, could see its wicked glow in Heidi's eyes.

Her lips twisted into a cruel smile as she approached, the candle in hand. Faron's heart pounded in his chest, his mind screaming for escape. The flame flickered as she brought it closer to him.

"Please! Please!" Faron begged, but his words were lost in the pain that soon followed.

She set the flame to his foot, the unbearable heat spreading instantly, sinking into his flesh. Faron's scream echoed through the room, raw and guttural, as he felt the flesh on his foot begin to burn. His eyes filled with tears, blurring his vision as pain shot up his leg. His body trembled, but the ropes kept him pinned, helpless.

Heidi watched, her gaze unfeeling, and her voice came again, thick with the power of Amir's presence. "I want you to experience the pain as I have experienced it."

Faron's world became a haze of fire and anguish. His body bucked against the pain, but he couldn't escape. He began to give way to unconsciousness, his vision dimming as the pain overwhelmed him.

***

Far from the house, Jazmin sat in a corner of a small, dimly lit room, her eyes red from crying. She hadn't heard from Haider in what felt like forever. Her mind raced, wondering where he was, what had happened to him.

But as she wiped away the tears, she noticed something—a movement. Haider was struggling, his body fighting against the ropes that bound him. His face contorted with pain, but determination flickered in his eyes.

With a final, desperate twist of his body, Haider broke free. He shoved Jazmin aside, his movements frantic as he stumbled toward the door, clutching Amir's family photograph in his hands.

"Coward!" Jazmin screamed after him, but Haider had already disappeared into the night.

At the police station, Haider stood before Owais, holding up the photograph. His hand shook, but his voice was steady, desperate.

"Do you recognize them?" he asked, his tone sharp, urgent.

Owais took the photo, his eyes widening in shock. He nodded slowly. "Yes! It's him!" His voice was laced with disbelief. "I warned them... I told them not to do it, but they didn't listen!"

Haider plead him. "Please, Owais. My father, my wife—they're gone. Amir took them. Please, you have to help me get them back. I know, I know it sounds crazy," Haider said, his voice urgent now. "But I've seen it with my own eyes. I've felt it. The way she looks at me now—it's not her. It's Amir."

Owais stared at him, confusion and disbelief clouding his features. "Are you telling me that Amir came back from the dead to kill people? And now he's inside your wife?" He shook his head in disbelief. "I can't... I can't believe that." But then something in Haider's pleading expression seemed to reach him, pushing through the layers of disbelief.

Haider's voice grew more desperate. "Just come with me. Please. You have to see it for yourself."

Back at Amir's house, the scene was one of unspeakable horror. Faron's lifeless body lay on the floor, his skin burnt and mutilated. Haider and Owais stood in the doorway, frozen, staring at the gruesome scene. Haider's heart shattered as he looked down at Faron's body.

He rushed forward, cradling Faron in his arms, his breath coming in ragged sobs. "No! no!" His voice cracked as tears began to fall. He pressed Faron's cold, burnt body to his chest, unable to comprehend the brutal scene before him.

A familiar sight caught his eye—a small, worn doll on a shelf. Haider's breath caught in his throat. Memories surged forward, crashing over him like a tidal wave. The warmth of his family, his sister's laughter echoing through their home, the way Fariya used to smile at him whenever she held that doll. The memories burned with a sharp, painful clarity. The family he had once known.

But the pain wasn't the only thing the doll reminded him of. A creeping sense of dread settled over him. The doll, this innocent object, had become a symbol of the horrors he was now facing. Heidi, with Amir's spirit coursing through her, had already taken so much. And as his gaze lingered on the doll, Haider knew, with a sickening certainty, that his sister would be next.

Chapter 11

Hellbound

At Faron's house, Fariya was playing in the living room when she suddenly left her toys behind and ran towards the kitchen where Shazia was cleaning the dining table. She looked up at her, concern written across her young face.

"Where are Mom and Dad? When will they return?" Fariya asked, her small voice tinged with worry.

Shazia paused for a moment, wiping her hands on the towel before answering, "They've gone to the hospital to see Haider. They'll be back soon."

Fariya's face twisted with confusion and a hint of sadness. "I want to meet Haider too. Every time they go out, they leave me alone at home. I think they don't love me."

Shazia knelt down to her, placing a comforting hand on her shoulder. "No, dear. They love you very much."

Suddenly, the lights in the house flickered. It was as if something was stirring. A knock echoed through the darkened house, sharp and unsettling. Shazia rose up, looking out the window. Her heart skipped a beat when she saw a figure standing in the dim light. It was Heidi. She quickly opened the door to let her in.

"Mom and Dad are back!" Fariya exclaimed from behind.

But the moment Heidi stepped inside, something in the air shifted. Fariya's joy was short-lived. Heidi moved swiftly, her hands reaching out, not to greet Shazia but to strangle her. Shazia gasped as her life was squeezed out of her, and with wide eyes, Fariya watched in horror, unable to move. Shazia collapsed to the floor, lifeless.

Terror surged through Fariya's veins. She ran, desperate to escape the danger. Heidi, however, followed her with unnerving calm, her eyes locked on the terrified child.

"Don't be afraid," says Heidi. "Come to me, darling. We're just playing a game."

Fariya's heart pounded as she dove behind the sofa, trying to hide.

Heidi's voice shifted. "Oh, you want to play hide and seek?" She paused. "My Amina loved that game too."

Fariya's breath hitched in her chest as Heidi moved closer. "One... two... three! I caught you!"

Just as Heidi's hands tightened around Fariya's throat, there was a sudden crash.

Haider and Owais burst into the house. Owais swung a heavy object at Heidi, and she staggered back, blood oozing from her head. But her body didn't falter.

Fariya, terrified, stumbled backward as Heidi's bloodied figure loomed. With a frantic glance at the men, she bolted to her room, slamming the door behind her, her breath shallow and fast.

Heidi turned slowly toward Owais and grabbed him by the neck, her supernatural strength overpowering him. "You are going to die just like the others," she hissed, her voice now fully consumed by the demon. With a primal roar, Heidi hurled Owais against the wall. The impact was deafening. His body slammed into the solid surface with terrifying force, and his head struck the wall with a sickening crack.

Haider's heart pounded in his chest as he watched Heidi, or whatever was left of her, advance toward him. His breath caught in his throat, and for a split second, the world around him seemed to slow. He had witnessed the destruction she had caused—Owais thrown like a ragdoll—and now, he was the one in her sights.

Heidi stormed toward him. Her movements were fluid, almost predatory, as she closed the distance between them. Haider barely had time to react before Heidi's hand shot out, grabbing him by the throat.

"You're not her," Haider whispered, his vision blurring. He could barely keep his balance, but Heidi's demonic voice roared in response.

"She's not here anymore," it snarled.

Haider tried to fight back and hit her with his leg. Heidi's grip was finally released. He pushed her aside with all his strength. Before he could run, Heidi grabbed and threw him to the kitchen, her face now twisted with the demonic rage of Amir.

"Don't worry, I won't let you die so easily," she said, her words dripping with venom.

"Amir!" Haider cried, his voice raw with pleading. "Stop! Please, just stop!"

"Why? Why should I stop? You are all evil! You all deserve to die!" Heidi screamed.

"I know they are evil, but I apologize for them! I'm sorry for what they did, but this revenge—it won't bring you peace. It won't heal you!"

Heidi's eyes burned with fury. "You don't understand," she spat. "We didn't do anything wrong! We begged for mercy, and they beat my wife to death. They burned me alive. No one helped us, no one cared. They are all evil! You are all evil!"

Heidi grabbed a nearby bottle of cooking oil from the counter. With a wicked smile, she poured it liberally across the floor, her hands steady despite the madness burning in her veins. "Look at it burn, Haider," she snarled. "Your house... your life... all of it. Just like they burned me."

With a swift motion, Heidi struck the match and let it fall onto the oily surface. The fire flared up immediately.

Haider's voice softened, filled with sorrow. "Think about your daughter, Amir. Fariya is just like your child. Don't do this to her!"

For a moment, something flickered in Heidi's eyes something fragile. Amir's mind was torn between the rage that controlled Heidi and the memories of the family he had once had. As if on cue, a flash of Amina's face appeared in Amir's mind. And then, just as quickly, the darkness returned.

Heidi's eyes narrowed as she turned to look at a photograph on the wall. It was Faron's face, the man who had burned Amir alive. The memory ignited a new wave of fury in Heidi. Grabbing a knife from the dining table, she moved closer to Haider.

"Kill me!" Haider cried, his voice raw and broken. "But please, I beg you—spare my wife, spare Fariya! They are innocent. They have nothing to do with this!"

Heidi turned the knife toward herself, pressing it against her stomach. "What are you doing?! Don't! Don't you dare!" Heidi shouted in Amir's demonic voice. Heidi's grip tightened around the knife as if fighting her own instincts. "No... You fool! You want to die too?"

For a brief, the humanity in her broke through. Her voice softened, and Haider could almost hear Heidi again, not the demon that had possessed her. "Is it really you?" he whispered, his heart heavy with the weight of his words.

She looked at him with sorrowful eyes and spoke, "Save Fariya. Leave this hell... please."

Haider, his heart shattering, shook his head. "I will not leave without you!"

Heidi closed her eyes, tears slipping down her face, and with a quiet, mournful whisper, she said, "Please, go. I love you." And then, with one swift movement, she drove the knife into her own stomach.

"No" Haider screamed, his heart breaking as he crawled toward her lifeless body. Tears streamed down his face as he held her, her body still warm, her life already slipping away.

Meanwhile, Fariya, hidden in the other room, was not safe. The flames had already started to creep through the door. She screamed as she saw the fire consume the walls around her.

"Fire! Fire!" Fariya cried, her voice filled with terror.

Haider, barely able to stand, made his way toward the door. His body was broken, his spirit crushed, but he had to reach Fariya. She was the last part of his family left.

He stumbled, collapsing against the doorframe, but pressed on. Each step was agony, he could hear Fariya's screams, and it drove him forward. The fire had reached Fariya now, the heat unbearable. Her skin blistered as the flames began to burn her. She cried out, her face contorted in pain. "It burns! It burns! Help me!"

Haider's heart broke with each of her cries. He could hear her, but he was too far away. He crawled desperately, but the fire seemed to get in his way at every turn. Then, the silence fell.

The haunting sound of Fariya's voice, once so close, vanished into the stillness. Panic clawed at him, but he forced himself to remain focused. He couldn't afford to stop. He couldn't let her fade into that empty silence.

Haider pushed himself forward, faster now, his body screaming in protest, but his will stronger than ever. The door was so close now—just a few more steps. And then, a faint sound. Fariya's voice. It was barely a whisper, but it was there. A lifeline. She was still alive. He wasn't too late.

With newfound strength, Haider burst through the door. The room smelled of smoke and burnt wood, the flames licking at the edges of the room, threatening to consume them both.

"Fariya!" Haider's voice cracked. He scanned the room for the girl and staggered in her direction once found.

Fariya's eyes flickered toward him, a faint glimmer of recognition, but she couldn't move.

He reached out, lifting her gently, his strength fueled by desperation. She gasped, clutching onto him weakly, her body trembling in his arms. He had to save her.

"You're going to be okay," he whispered, more to himself than to her, but the words were all he had. "We're getting out of here."

They reached the door. Outside air—sharp contrast to the suffocating smoke behind them. He stepped out into the open. The cool night air hitting his face like a wave. The fire raged behind them, but it didn't matter. They were free.

Fariya's weak hand gripped his, her breath shallow but steadying. She looked up at him, her eyes filled with a mixture of relief and gratitude.

Manufactured by Amazon.ca
Acheson, AB